Can you see him? My kitten?

His long whiskers too?

He's the best EVER pet.

He's a wish that came true!

Imagine him, quick!

Have you imagined enough?

Oh, good! You can see him!

It's Squishy McFluff!

Squishy McFluff

The Invisible Cat

Secret Santa

by *Pip Jones*

Illustrated by *Ella Okstad*

ff

FABER & FABER

A cold winter's day

was only just dawning.

'Hey, Squishy!' squealed Ava.

'IT'S CHRISTMAS MORNING!'

'Not yet . . .' Mummy called,

from her bedroom next door.

'Still four days to go.

Can't we all sleep some more?

'Invisible kittens

need plenty of rest.

4

Back to bed. It's too EARLY.

Mummy knows best!'

But, hearing that Ava and

Squish couldn't settle,

Mum tramped

down the stairs . . .

and put on the kettle.

In the kitchen, Mum asked:

'Now, do you remember

'How good you both need to be

all through December?'

'Oh, yes!' Ava answered.

'We'll be helpful, Mum.

'We know if we're naughty then

Santa won't come!'

'Lovely!' Mum said.

'We've a few bits to buy

'At the Christmas Bazaar:

some tinsel, a pie,

'A wedge of the cheese that your

dad likes to eat . . .'

Ava said: 'Mum,

will McFluff get a treat?'

'He can have ONE

invisible fish,' Mum replied.

'Now, let's get your coat on,

it's freezing outside.'

9

At the Christmas Bazaar,

a choir was singing.

The tunes were so festive,

with bells softly ringing.

Ava gazed all around,

then she whispered: 'Wowee!

'Just look at that, Squish!

What a huge Christmas tree!'

The giant tree's fairy lights

glittered and glimmered,

The beautiful garlands

sparkled and shimmered

And, right at the top,

a star shone so bright . . .

But Ava said: 'Crumpets!

That doesn't look right . . .'

The star was all wonky!

Completely askew!

Ava said: 'Squishy,

this really won't do!

'Perhaps we should fix it.

We promised we would

'Try ever so hard

to be helpful and good.'

So, while Mum was choosing

a cinnamon flan,

Squish (silently) miaowed

a **magnificent** plan!

McFluff jumped on a branch

and started to climb.

He scrambled halfway

up the tree in no time.

When he got near the top,

Ava said with a moan:

'Oh bother! You can't

reach the star

on your own!

'I can't climb up too, Squish,

it looks far too high!'

'But we have to do something!

What else can we try?'

At the top of the tree,

McFluff had a think.

He suddenly grinned.

He gave Ava a wink.

16

And while Mum was buying

a giant fruit cake,

Squish pawed at the trunk

to say: 'Give it a shake!'

'Of course!' Ava cried,

with a smile on her face.

'I'll **wobble** the tree 'til the

star's back in place!'

She shook the tree's trunk

with all of her might.

'No, STOP!' yelled a lady,

her face going white.

The star didn't straighten!

Instead it just . . . FELL!

Then baubles and beads

started tumbling as well.

AND SO DID MCFLUFF!

He was plummeting fast.

'THE STAR!' a man shouted,

but Ava pushed past

And **just** caught her precious

invisible cat . . .

While the star fell on top of

a cake with a SPLAT!

Ava said: 'Phew!

That was close, little one!'

McFluff smiled, but Mummy shrieked:

'What have you DONE?!'

'We were helping!' said Ava.

'The star wasn't straight.'

Mum sighed as she started

to redecorate

The towering tree, with its

baubles and beads –

'It's lovely to help,' Mum said,

'but, Ava, please

'Would you and that kitten

of yours make a vow

'To just "help" me at home . . .

starting from NOW!'

Very early, the next day,

Daddy yawned loudly.

'I put jam on your toast for you,'

Ava said proudly.

'So helpful,' said Dad,

slowly stirring his tea.

'But I wish you'd slept later

than quarter to three!'

'Oh, sorry!' said Ava.

'We were fast asleep, then

'We woke up 'cos we thought

       it was Christmas again!'

'Just three days to go!'

    said Mum, cuddling Roo.

'I'll need your help, Ava.

We have lots to do!

'I'll make some mince pies

while Daddy is napping.

'Perhaps you could help me

by doing some wrapping?

'There's SO much to wrap.

Look! Everything here!

'But don't wake up Dad,

'cos he's tired. Is that clear?'

'Oh goodie!' said Ava.

'Squish, this will be brill!

'Let's start with that new cap

for Great Grandad Bill!'

They wrapped up the hat

(and enjoyed it a lot).

They wrapped up a big gnome

for Mad Nana Dot.

They wrapped loads of candles

and photos in frames,

Socks, fluffy slippers,

books and board games.

'Aw, we've finished already!'

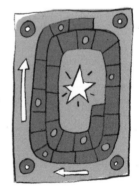

Ava grumpily said.

But Squishy McFluff

gave a shake of his head . . .

'You're right, Squish!' said Ava.

'How silly of me!'

'Mum said: "Wrap EVERYTHING."

Next . . . the settee!'

So they wrapped the settee,

and both of the tables,

They wrapped up the TV

(not touching the cables),

They wrapped up the lamps

and then, taking great care

Not to wake Daddy,

they wrapped his armchair!

Mummy came back from

the kitchen . . .

and GASPED!

'Did we do a good job?'

Ava happily asked.

'You might have . . .' said Mum,

'. . . overdone it a tad!

'Now, you get your pencils

while I unwrap

Dad.

'I think you have both "helped"

enough with the chores.

'You've a letter to write . . .

and it's for Santa Claus.'

'Yippee!' Ava cried,

and she found Dad's best pen.

She ran to her bedroom

with Squishy, and then

Ava stared at the paper,

so blank and so white.

She stroked McFluff's ears . . .

and she started to write.

The days came and went.

Chestnuts were roasted.

The cards were all sent.

Santa's letter was posted.

Mum unwrapped the fridge

(McFluff got the blame)

And finally, FINALLY,

Christmas Eve came!

Ava and Squishy

both had a long bath.

They put a mince pie

and some milk on the hearth.

The clock in the hallway

started to chime.

'Right, Ava,' said Mummy.

'Upstairs! It's bedtime.'

'But we want to SEE Santa!'

Ava told Mum.

'You MUST sleep,' said Mummy,

'or else he won't come!

'So let's tuck you in,

you're already yawning.

'Night night, and I'll see you

first thing in the MORNING.'

Well, McFluff had a plan –

It would work like a charm!

'Good thinking,' said Ava.

'Let's set the alarm!'

Ava set it for midnight,

then they both fell asleep.

And several hours later . . .

BEEP! BEEP! BEEP! BEEP!

BANG! CLANK! CRASH!

'Bother!'

CLINK!

'Oh dear!'

THUMP!

Ava gasped! All the clattering

made Squishy JUMP!

They crept into the lounge.

They peeped over a shelf,

And that's when they both saw . . .

SANTA HIMSELF!

Santa's beard was silvery white,

and it twinkled!

His face was so smiley and

cheerfully wrinkled.

His boots were all sooty,

his red suit was felt

And around his plump middle

he wore a black belt.

Squishy's eyes were so wide.

Ava was beaming

But, to be **certain**

she wasn't just dreaming,

She blinked both her eyes and

pinched her own wrist,

Then said: 'Santa! So we're NOT

on your naughty list?'

Well, Santa Claus gave

a quick wink of his eye.

'No one's perfect!' he said.

'But I know that you try.

'And one thing that sets all

good children apart

'Is not to be perfect . . .

but to have a kind heart.'

By the fire were presents

in all shapes and sizes.

A wonderful mountain of

gift-wrapped surprises!

Ava gazed at the parcels,

piled up so high,

Yet she looked a bit glum

and she gave a long sigh.

Squishy McFluff gave a sad

(silent) miaow . . .

'What's wrong?' Santa asked,

crinkling his brow.

'It's just . . .' Ava whispered,

'what would have been better . . .'

'Ho ho!' Santa cried.

'Yes, I DID get your letter . . .

'Your handwriting's lovely,

    you must be quite proud!'

Santa took out the letter,

    then read it aloud:

'Dear Santa, I'm Ava!
   Oh, I do hope you will
Drop by my house
   (it's the one on the hill).
Mum said, as we tried
   to be helpful and pleasant,
I could write you a letter
   and ask for a present.

So I thought about what
   sort of gift I would like.
A scooter, perhaps . . .
   or a lovely new bike.
But what I desperately want,
   well, it's more of a wish . . .
Just ONCE, I'd like somebody
   else to SEE SQUISH!'

63

Ava sighed. 'I just love him

so much,' she explained.

'Well of course you do, Ava!'

Santa exclaimed.

'All that fluffy white fur,

and his tiny pink nose!

'Yes, he's ever so sweet . . .!'

Ava . . . just . . . FROZE.

'You mean you CAN see him?'

she finally said.

'Of course I can!' Santa was

nodding his head.

'Prove it!' said Ava.

So Santa asked: 'How?'

'Just tell me,' said Ava,

'where's Squishy right NOW?'

Squish started bouncing

and darting around.

Santa laughed, then he said,

as he knelt on the ground:

'Behind you, behind you!

Mind where you stand!

'He's right by your shoe!

Now he's sniffing your hand!

'He's climbed on your shoulder!

His tail's in your EAR!

'Look harder! Turn quicker!

No, not THERE . . . he's here!'

Santa leant forwards,

then on to his mitten

Leapt Ava's not-quite-so-

invisible kitten.

Ava giggled and squealed.

She gave Santa a hug.

(The fur on his collar was

ever so snug.)

'Thank you, oh thank you!'

she said with a smile.

'You've made me SO happy,

please stay for a while.'

Santa Claus chortled:

'I'd love to, my dear!

'But I can't – it's my busiest
night of the year!'
Santa waved them to bed,
saying: 'Go on! It's late!'

. . . And Ava and Squish slept

'til quarter past EIGHT!

In the lounge, all the presents

were in the same place

But there was no sign of Santa,

not one little trace.

No footprints were left in

the lounge, or the hall.

'Oh, Squishy,' said Ava,

'did we imagine it all?'

Ava read from a label:

'Especially for Squish,
Enjoy the world's
BIGGEST invisible fish!'

And behind that huge box,

right there on the floor,

Was a letter she'd posted

just three days before!

It was crumpled and rumpled

and damp from the snow,

With a black, sooty hand print

and, just below,

RECEI
THE NOR
POLE

'RECEIVED: THE NORTH POLE'

some big letters read.

'It really DID happen!'

Ava happily said.

'No one will believe us,

but we KNOW it's true!

'Merry Christmas, dear Squishy!

And Merry Christmas . . .

To YOU!'